Oops, Pig!

PUFFIN BOOKS

Published by the Penguin Group
Penguin Books Ltd, 27 Wrights Lane, London W8 5TZ, England
Penguin Books USA Inc., 375 Hudson Street, New York, New York 10014, USA
Penguin Books Australia Ltd, Ringwood, Victoria, Australia
Penguin Books Canada Ltd, 10 Alcorn Avenue, Toronto, Ontario, Canada M4V 3B2
Penguin Books (NZ) Ltd, Cnr Rosedale and Airborne Roads, Albany, Auckland, New Zealand

Penguin Books Ltd, Registered Offices: Harmondsworth, Middlesex, England

First published in the USA by Random House, Inc. 1998
Published in Puffin Books 1998
1 3 5 7 9 10 8 6 4 2

Made and printed in Great Britain by Saxon Profile Press

British Library Cataloguing in Publication Data
A CIP catalogue record for this book is available from the British Library

ISBN 0–140–56469–1

BABE
The Sheep Pig™

Oops, Pig!

By Shana Corey

Illustrated by Donald Cook

Based on the character Babe created by Dick King-Smith

The sun comes up.
"Quack-a-doodle-doo!"
shouts the duck.

Babe is still asleep.

Wake up, sleepyhead!

Time for breakfast!
Pancakes for the farmer.

Hay for the horses.

Feed for the chickens.

And slops for Babe!

Time for chores.

Gather the eggs, Babe.

Milk the cow, Babe.

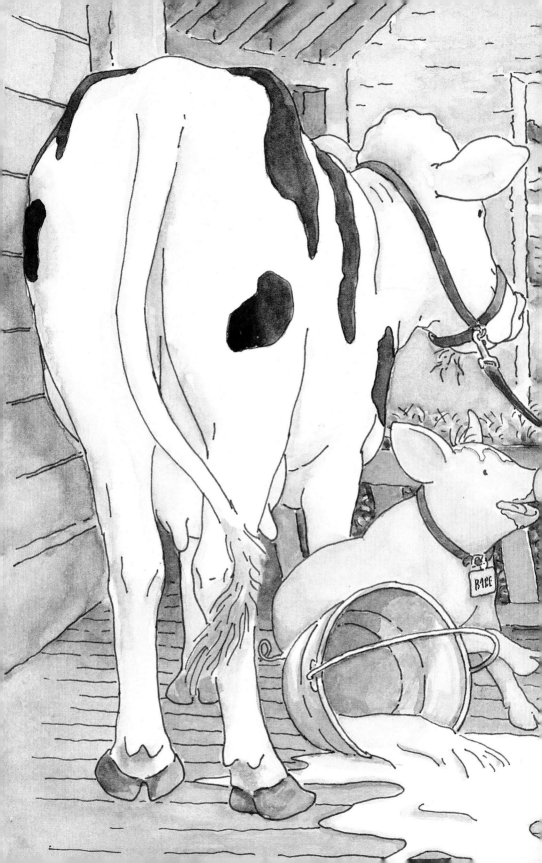

Uh-oh!

Weed the garden, Babe.

Oh dear!

"Babe! What a mess
you have made!"

Babe wants to help.
What can he do?

Babe can herd sheep!

"Good job, Pig,"

says the farmer.